Stories from Different Countries

Selected by Wendy Body

Contents

29

Longman

Edinburgh Gate
Harlow, Essex

Why Do Dogs Chase Cars?

A modern myth from West Africa

Everyone in West Africa knows why dogs chase cars.

Some time ago, when cars first came to the roads, a donkey, a goat and a dog took a ride in a taxi. They were off out of town, to the villages where they lived.

When they reached the first village, the donkey tapped the driver on the shoulder. "This is where I'm getting out, driver," he said. "How much?"

"Three thousand francs," said the driver. The donkey paid up and on went the goat and the dog in the taxi.

Soon the goat asked to be dropped off.

"How much?" he asked.

"Three thousand francs," said the driver. The goat didn't hang about. He jumped from the taxi and scampered off into the bush.

At long last the dog got to where he wanted to go.

"How much?" said the dog.

"Three thousand francs," said the driver. The dog held up a five thousand franc note. The driver grabbed the note, and drove off down the road roaring with laughter.

So now you know why a donkey, a goat and a dog all do different things when a car comes down the road.

Donkeys just stay right where they are. They let the driver go round them. They know they paid up. They've done nothing wrong, so they've got nothing to be ashamed of.

The moment a car comes down the road and there's a goat around, it'll scamper off as fast as it can because it knows that it didn't pay the fare and the driver is looking for his money.

But dogs spend their whole time chasing cars looking for the driver who once cheated them.

From *South and North, East and West*
by Michael Rosen

The Tale of Two Frogs

A fable from Japan

Long, long ago, two frogs lived in the country of Japan.
One frog lived in a very nice ditch near Osaka, a small
town which was not very far from the sea. The other
frog lived in a pretty little stream near Kyoto. Kyoto was
the large city where the Emperor of Japan had his
palace.

The two frogs had never met because they lived such a
long way apart. But they had one thing in common: they
both wanted to go travelling. The frog from Kyoto
wanted to see Osaka, the town by the sea. The frog
from Osaka wanted to see Kyoto – the city where the
Emperor lived.

One fine morning in spring, both frogs woke up with
the same thought: "Today I shall go travelling!"
They both set off on the long road which ran
between Osaka and Kyoto: one frog from his
ditch in Osaka and the other from his stream
in Kyoto. They did not know how far they
had to travel but they each hopped
along full of the joys of spring.
There was something else
they did not know: half-way
between Osaka and Kyoto
there was a big mountain
which they would
have to climb.

When the frog from Osaka got to his side of the mountain he stopped to rest. When the frog from Kyoto got to his side of the mountain he stopped to rest, too. Then they both set off to hop to the top. It took them a long while but at last they reached the top of the mountain – and there they met. Both frogs were very tired so they found a nice spot under a rock to rest and to chat.

The two frogs were very pleased when they found out that they had something in common. They chatted about how they wanted to travel and how they wanted to see places which were different from where they lived. Both of them also said how tired they were.

And then the frog from Osaka said: "It's a shame we are not taller. If we were, I could see Kyoto from here and you could see Osaka. Then we could both decide if we wanted to carry on travelling."

The frog from Kyoto thought about this and then he said: "I know what to do. We stand up on our back legs and hold on to each other to stop us falling over. That way, you will be able to see Kyoto and I will be able to see Osaka."

The frog from Osaka thought that this was a very good idea. They both stood on their back legs, stretched themselves up and hung on to each other to keep their balance. The frog from Osaka faced Kyoto and the frog from Kyoto faced Osaka.

But there was one thing these silly frogs forgot. When they stood up, their big round eyes were at the back of their heads. They were facing the places they wanted to visit … but they were looking at the places they had come from!

"Oh dear," the frog from Osaka said sadly. "Kyoto looks just like Osaka. I'm not going all the way to see a place which is exactly the same as the one I live in."

"And I'm not going all the way to Osaka when it looks exactly the same as Kyoto!" the frog from Kyoto replied. "We should have stayed at home, my friend!"

The two foolish frogs said goodbye to each other. Then they set off back to their homes, thinking that Kyoto and Osaka were exactly the same and never knowing how different the places really were!

Based on 'The Two Frogs', retold by Mark Cohen in *The Puffin Book of Fabulous Fables*

The Painter and the Judge

A traditional story from China

Once there was a judge who was very mean. Everyone knew that to get him to listen to you, you had to go to him secretly and give him huge amounts of money. And even then he might just take the money and still not give you a fair hearing. People often felt that he had cheated them.

One day the judge heard there was a painter in town who could paint the most wonderful pictures. The judge found the man and gave him a roll of white paper to get working on.

"Paint me a beautiful picture," said the judge.

At first the painter didn't want to. He knew how mean the judge was and said to himself, "I might do a lot of work on this painting and end up not getting paid."

"I'm very busy at the moment," he said. "I just don't have the time." But the judge begged him, saying, "I shall put it up in a place where all the most important people in town will see it."

In the end the painter said he would do a picture for the judge.

The next day, he came to the judge's house with the roll of paper.

"Wise One, I have finished the painting."

The judge was delighted but when he unrolled the paper, he couldn't see any picture on it. Instead, there were a few words: 'Cows on Grass'.

The judge stared at the blank piece of paper.

"But where's the grass?" he said.

"The cows have eaten it," answered the painter.

"But then where are the cows?" said the judge.

"Well," said the painter, "seeing as they'd eaten all the grass, there wasn't much point in them hanging around any more, was there? So they went."

From *South and North, East and West* by Michael Rosen

The Seal Wife

A Scottish folk tale

Magnus, a young fisherman, sees the seal people dancing on the shore. Rushing to join them, he frightens them and they pull on their sealskins and go back to the sea. All except one beautiful girl. Magnus steals her sealskin and claims her as his wife …

In no time word went round the village of the strange and beautiful woman Magnus had taken to wife, and soon they came to visit. One after another his friends and their wives called and, in return, invited him to bring his wife to the village. But Magnus had no time for them, and his wife sat silent, shaking her head. She refused to leave the cottage by the shore, and gradually Magnus realised she would neither set foot on the road to the village, nor on the path to the hills.

He saw then the way to keep her always with him. Setting out early one morning he climbed to the top of the hill behind the house and hid her sealskin under a cairn of stones amongst the heather where she would not go. For long months he watched as she wandered restlessly along the beach, climbing among the rock pools, searching, searching. But gradually she seemed to settle to life in the cottage and to accept that there was no returning to her own people.

Time passed and children were born to Magnus and his wife. There were five sons, four of them tall, sturdy children with straw fair hair and blue eyes, but the youngest, whom his mother loved the best, was small and slim with soft silvery hair and sea-dark eyes.

Magnus loved them all and doted on his wife. She in turn seemed happy to settle down with him in the cottage. She cooked and kept the place clean and shining and would have seemed like any other wife, but for her strange moods, and the songs she sang as she worked.

They enchanted Magnus. Sometimes, singing to the children, her voice was soft and gentle as the breeze on a summer night. At other times she sang strange wild songs with the high keening note of the north wind across a winter sea. It was at those times she spent hours wandering by herself along the tideline, gazing out across the water, as if enraptured by some sound that Magnus himself could not hear. He was afraid of those times, but as the years went by they became fewer and he learned to forget his fear.

Then one day when Magnus was away fishing with the three older boys, the two younger ones went to play on the hillside above the cottage. They were running and hiding amongst the rocks when the smallest child found the sealskin. Never had he touched anything so beautiful. He snatched it up and, followed by his brother, ran back to the cottage.

"Mother, mother. See what I have found. See the bonny fur, it is so soft and silky."

She dropped the dishes on the table, took the fur from her son and, stroking his hair, gazed long into his sea-dark eyes. Then slowly, followed by the little ones, she left the cottage. Lifting her head until her silver hair streamed in the fresh sea-wind she walked down across the sand. Away to her left she could see Magnus and the boys heading back towards the beach.

Quickly she turned to the two small boys and kissed them, then quicker still, she turned away, and lifting her skirts, ran down to the water.

Too late, Magnus hauled on the oars. He shouted from the boat, seeing her pull the sealskin around her shoulders and dive into the creaming surf. Briefly her head showed above the waves, sleek and wet, and, as he and the children watched, another seal came to meet her and together the two swam out, bobbing and dancing on the waves.

They watched, staring at the water until the seals vanished.

They watched for many years, but she never came back again. Sometimes, though, in the hour of sunset and the quiet of an ebbing tide, as Magnus walked along the shore he would stop and listen. From far off, beyond the sound of the sea and the wind, there came a sweet, wild song. And only he and his youngest son could hear it.

Retold by Moira Miller in *A Kist O'Whistles*

The Merman

A traditional tale from Tobago

There was once a young woman called Margaret who was so beautiful that her fame spread to every county in the island of Tobago and many songs were composed about her. Margaret was also an excellent swimmer, equally at home in river and sea.

She was swimming in the sea one day when a man suddenly appeared beside her. He was young and handsome and soon they were chatting like two old friends. After a while the man said to Margaret, "There are some lovely underwater gardens not far from here but you would have to be a strong swimmer to get there. Are you a good swimmer, Margaret?"

Margaret was taken aback when he spoke her name for she had not told it to him. However, she replied, "I have been told that I'm like a fish in water."

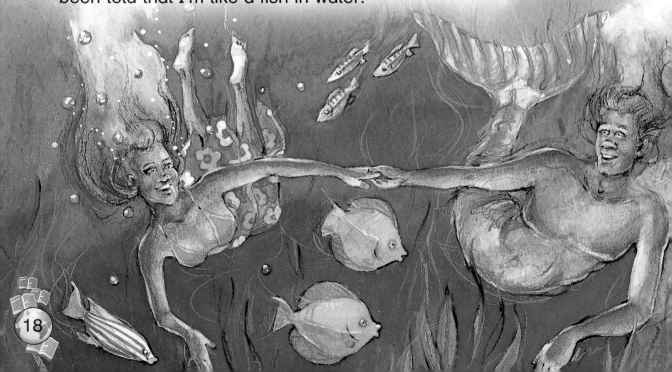

"You have no fear of the sea then?" he enquired.

"I fear the sea as much as I fear the land. No more, no less," said Margaret.

"Right then, let us see what kind of fish you are," he said. And seizing her hand he dived so swiftly that before she knew it she was in a large hall with walls of coral, festooned with sea-green vines. The rooms which led off from the hall were a sight to behold and were paved with marble floors that shone like glass.

There Margaret saw her companion fully for the first time and realised that he was no mortal man but a merman. She was not afraid of him for he continued to treat her with the utmost courtesy. She herself had an open curiosity about everything and was fascinated by the spectacular undersea gardens which the merman

showed her. There was so much to see that Margaret was surprised when he said to her, "You have been with us for three days. Would you like to stay and be my true companion, Margaret?"

"Three days! Why, I thought I had been here only a few hours. How is it that I have neither eaten not slept and I feel none the worse for it?" asked Margaret.

"Time feels different here because there is no change of light and also because of the flow of water. But tell me Margaret, will you stay?"

Margaret did not know what to do or say. To tell the truth she was in love with this gentle man of the sea who treated her like a princess. But to stay with him meant that she would never see her folk and friends again. She was clever enough not to provoke his anger with a hasty refusal so she said, "Let me think it about it for a little longer."

Now that she knew he wanted her to stay Margaret was careful about what she consumed. She had once been told that these beings could bewitch a person by giving them certain things to eat and drink. So she drank only clear water and ate only sea-grapes. Finally she told the merman that she wished to return to her world. "I am likely to die from homesickness if I stay with you," she said. And since he loved her truly he let her go and took her up through what seemed to be a special tunnel to the beach near her village. But before they parted he gave her a beautiful stone which reflected the colours of the rainbow when it was held up to the sun.

"It will ensure a long and full life, and good fortune will be with you always," said the merman when he gave it to her.

And so it was. She lived to be over one hundred years old and she never lost her beauty. She never moved from her village near the sea and asked to be buried at sea when she died.

From *Mouth Open, Story Jump Out* by Grace Hallworth

The Pupu Pool

A story from New Zealand

For both Mum and Dad, going to the reef was a good excuse to meet our friends and relations. It was almost a family affair.

My sisters and I, we made straight for the pupu pool.

The pool was very long but not very deep. At its deepest the water was waist high. The reef around it was fringed with long waving seaweed. Small transparent fish swam among the waving leaves, and little crabs scurried across the floor of the pool. The pupus glided calmly along the sides of the reef. Once, we saw a starfish, inching its way into a dark crack.

But our most beautiful discovery was a delicate seahorse, magical and serene, shimmering among the red kelp and riding the swirls of the sea's current.

My sisters and I, we wanted to take it home.

"If you take it from the sea it will die," Dad told us. "Leave it here in its own home, for the sea gives it life and beauty."

And Dad went on, giving us our first lesson about treating the sea with aroha.

"Kids, you must take from the sea only the kai you need and only the amount you need to please your bellies. If you take more, then it is waste. Why waste food? Best to leave it in the sea for when you will need it the next time. The sea is good to us, it gives us kai to eat. As long as we respect it, it will continue to favour us. If you lift a stone from its lap as you search for shellfish, return the stone to where it was. Try not to break pieces of the reef, for it is the home of many kai moana. And do not leave litter behind you when you leave the sea …"

Our father, he taught us to respect the sea and to have reverence for the life held in its waters. As we collected pupus, we would remember his words. And whenever the seahorse peeked shyly at us from behind a curtain of kelp, we felt glad that we had left it in the pool to delight us …

One day, we went again to the reef. We were in a happy mood. The sun was shining and skipping its beams like bright stones across the water. But when we got to the reef, it was deserted. There were no people dotting the sea with their sacks, no loud calls of welcome from them.

Dad frowned. He saw our friends and relations clustered on the beach. There were many of them, staring out towards the reef.

"Something's wrong," he said.

He stopped the truck and we walked with him towards the people. They were silent and sad.

"The water too cold?" Dad asked, trying to joke.

Nobody answered him.

"Is there a shark out there?" Dad continued. Someone pointed to a sign. It had been put up during the night. Dad elbowed through the crowd to read it.

"What does it say, Dad?" I asked. His fists were clenched and his eyes were angry. Then his fists unclenched and his eyes became sad.

"It says that it is dangerous to take sea food from the reef."

"Why, Dad?"

"They've run a sewer pipe out there, son. The sea is polluted. If we eat the sea food we may get sick."

My sisters and I were silent for a while.

"No more pupus, Dad?"

"No more, son."

"And the seahorse, Dad? Will it be all right?"

He shrugged his shoulders.

We walked back to the truck. Behind us, an old woman began to cry out a tangi to the reef. It was a very sad song for such a beautiful day. While she was singing, Dad stopped and bowed his head. When the tangi had finished, he whispered: "We have been unkind to the

26

sea. We have poisoned the land and now we feed our poison into the water. We have lost our aroha for the sea and our respect for its life."

He started the truck. We turned homeward.

In my mind I caught a vision of pupus crawling among polluted rocks. I saw a starfish encrusted with ugliness.

And flashing through dead waving seaweed was a beautiful seahorse, fragile and dream-like, searching frantically for clean and crystal waters.

By Witi Ihimaera
From *The Magpies Said*

The Ghost

A ghostly tale from India

There was much rejoicing in the house of the merchant, for his youngest son was to marry. His wife-to-be, a lovely young woman from the neighbouring town, was eagerly awaited by her in-laws. She travelled in a palanquin after the wedding, while her husband rode on ahead to welcome her home.

The palanquin-bearers became tired during the journey and rested under a bilva tree. The young bride stepped out of the palanquin to stretch her limbs. Just then the ghost who lived in the tree saw her and fell in love with her. The palanquin-bearers continued the journey and carried the bride to her new home. The ghost was left in the tree looking longingly after her.

A few weeks after his marriage, it was decided that the young man should go far away to the big town. He should establish a business and hopefully bring riches to his family. Sadly, the young man said goodbye to his wife and promised to return as soon as possible. The ghost had been watching all this and now decided to carry out his plan.

Some days later he took on the form of the young man and came to the house. Everyone was surprised at the early return. He explained that it was not the right time for his work and that he had decided to delay starting his business by a few months. So he was welcomed back and his young wife was especially happy.

The days passed into weeks, the weeks into months and the months into years. The household carried out its functions. Everything seemed to be going very well. Suddenly one day, the young man returned. He had been successful in his work and brought back the wealth he had earned.

You can imagine the shock that the family suffered. There were now two young men, both claiming to be the actual son of the parents and the husband of the young wife. Neither his parents nor his wife could decide which of the two was the genuine young man since they were identical in appearance.

The two young men fought, abused and accused each other of being a fraud. Everyone in the family was very upset. No one could understand how to solve this problem. So they all went to the head of the guild of merchants to ask his opinion.

The head of the guild listened carefully. After thinking for a while, he sent for a small leather bag and said to both men that whichever of the two could turn himself into a tiny person and enter the bag was obviously the genuine young man. The real young man said that it was impossible. The ghost on the other hand laughed and immediately shrank and entered the bag. The head of the guild quickly tied the mouth of the bag and then dropped it into a well.

Thus the family were rid of the ghost. The young man was welcomed home, warmly.

**From *Indian Tales*
by Romila Thapar**